ASCEND

SLEEPING DRAGONS BOOK 6

OPHELIA BELL

Ascend
Copyright © 2014 Ophelia Bell
Cover Art Designed by Dawné Dominique
Photograph Copyrights © Fotolio.com, DepositPhotos.com, CanStock.com

Published by Ophelia Bell
UNITED STATES

ISBN-13: 978-1544615066
ISBN-10: 154461506X

ALSO BY OPHELIA BELL

SLEEPING DRAGONS SERIES

Animus

Tabula Rasa

Gemini

Shadows

Nexus

Ascend

RISING DRAGONS SERIES

Night Fire

Breath of Destiny

Breath of Memory

Breath of Innocence

Breath of Desire

Breath of Love

Breath of Flame & Shadow

Breath of Fate

Sisters of Flame

IMMORTAL DRAGONS SERIES

Dragon Betrayed

Dragon Blues

Dragon Void

STANDALONE EROTIC TALES

After You
Out of the Cold

OPHELIA BELL TABOO

Burying His Desires

•

Blackmailing Benjamin
Betraying Benjamin
Belonging to Benjamin

•

Casey's Secrets
Casey's Discovery
Casey's Surrender

Love will release you.

CHAPTER ONE

Corey stood in the center of the corridor staring at the massive green jade double door. He felt like a fool for deciding to go through with this—*date*—or whatever it was. As much sexual eye candy as he'd witnessed over the last few hours and as frustrated as he was as a result, he'd always considered himself the kind of guy who cared about more substance in his partners.

It had been Kris, finally, who had changed Corey's mind about going through with this. Kris who had made him understand the unique nature of these people their team had awakened. He had a hard time thinking of them as anything other than people, in spite of the fantastic shapes he'd seen them take. He'd drawn a few of his own conclusions, too. Very unscientific conclusions, probably, but he had a feeling Erika or the others might agree with him.

In spite of the very sexual nature of their new friends, each one of them ultimately had seemed human to him in one very particular way. They weren't mindless sex fiends. That realization had come, ironically, in the middle of watching the only orgy Corey thought he could ever stomach. He'd stayed to man the camera for as long as he could endure, but in that span of time he'd seen how attentive and caring each of the dragons had been to his or her lovers.

Corey had been with his share of lovers, all women, but only with one of them had he ever come close to feeling what he'd seen in all the dragons' eyes during the course of that night. It made him ache in a much deeper place than his balls to think he could have that again with a woman. He just hoped this particular woman wouldn't end up finding him wanting after a few months and leave him for a richer man.

Hell, she might hate him from the beginning, but he'd been on plenty bad dates and the world hadn't ended as a result. Shit, he hoped the world *didn't end* if this went badly. He'd seen some of the magic the dragons could do and wondered how much more they were capable of when full-up. *Like Kris shooting fireworks from his fingertips*, Corey thought. If only a normal orgasm could feel *that* good. Just being in the room at that point would've been enough to make Corey's cock hard as a rock, if it hadn't been already.

Corey wiped his damp palms on his pants and took a tentative step forward. Should he knock? Or should he just go in? All it had taken Dimitri was a touch to the doors of that chamber and they'd opened up, like he'd done it with the power of a thought.

"Fuck it," Corey muttered and rapped the knuckles of one hand lightly on the carved jade figure that graced the front of the door. He only had a second to regret which part of the woman's image he'd managed to choose to touch before the doors both swung inward. He hurriedly raked shaky fingers through his hair and wished fervently that he'd had more time to prepare—to bring her flowers or something. As it was, all he was showing up with was a raging hard-on that hadn't subsided in hours. He'd finally just written it off as something he'd have to live with for the time being.

He stood on the threshold, gazing around at the interior of a massive chamber easily the size of the throne room. It was completely lit, and at the far end was a huge bed with four columns of carved jade rising from each corner.

He almost didn't see her, as small as she was relative to the scope of the room and the bed. When he finally realized she was there, seated serenely in the center of the bed, he raised a hand and gave her a tentative wave.

"Ah…Sorry I'm late."

She only nodded and raised a hand to gesture for him to come forward. Once he was a few paces in, she made another slight gesture and the doors swept closed behind him.

Corey's heart pounded as he looked over his shoulder at his only means of escape. But escape from what, exactly? He swallowed his anxiety and turned forward again to take a good look at this *dragon queen* he was somehow so irrationally afraid of. He stepped a few more paces into the room, keeping his eyes on her. She seemed so placid, sitting there, just watching him come to her. Halfway into the room he stopped, deciding that was far enough. If she wanted him, she'd have to meet him the rest of the way.

Now that he was closer he could see her very clearly. His uncertainty replaced by cautious interest in the lovely figure.

She was a petite young woman with skin so fair it glowed and thick black curls that fell past her breasts. She had the same Asian features as Kris, though much more lovely and feminine compared to the guide's. Of course, Corey reminded himself, she was Kris's sister. Her bright green eyes watched him take her in. He only made a cursory glance of her body, quickly shifting his eyes back up when he realized she was stark naked.

Of course she's naked, dummy. This is like the dragon nudist colony. Though he supposed dragons might not normally wear clothes when they were being…well…*dragons.*

She frowned and finally spoke. "Do you not find me pleasing to look upon, human?" Her voice sounded light and smooth, and carried easily across the expanse of the room to his ears.

Corey cleared his throat. "Oh, trust me, I find you spectacular."

"Then why won't you come to me?"

Corey stood blinking at her. She sounded genuinely confused by his hesitation, but not in the way he'd have expected someone with the title of "Queen" to sound. She cocked her head in an endearing way, waiting for him to respond.

"I'm not sure what you expect so I'm just being cautious, if that's alright. I'm not in the habit of just jumping into bed with a pretty girl the first time we meet, I don't care how kinky you normally get with your lovers."

"What can I do to appease your reservations?"

Corey took a deep, calming breath through his nose and rubbed the back of his neck. Eyebrows raised slightly, he said, "Well, you *could* start by telling me your name. Then maybe we just talk a little?"

"My name is Racha. And you are Corey. My brother told me of you before you arrived at my door."

"Oh? What did good old Kris have to say?"

"That you are not like the other humans, but I think you are."

"And what makes you think that?"

"You're here, and you want me."

Now *there* was the Queen he'd expected. Her assertion irritated him, which he hated because she wasn't lying. Except it was a hollow want he felt, not the deep abiding need he'd seen in the others' eyes, particularly Kris's just before he'd made love to Issa for the first time.

"Maybe I just don't want you enough," he said.

Racha grew thoughtful. Her gaze slid over his body and paused at his hips before moving back to his eyes.

"Prove you don't. Take off your clothes."

Heat rushed to Corey's face at the command. The hell he'd strip naked. Well, he might have just to prove the point, except being naked in front of her would only prove the opposite.

"I have a better idea. Why don't you put something *on* and we can talk about this like two sane people who…I dunno… actually get to know each other before fucking."

CHAPTER TWO

Racha was fascinated by the human's reluctance to bed her. All the others had participated so enthusiastically. She was brimming with the power the others had fed to her and could taste how willingly the humans had given of themselves. All except for this one. That he'd resisted participating thus far either meant he was physically incapable or he had some other aversion to the act. And the evidence of his body's willingness was as plain as day.

Tired of the vast distance still between them, she gave in and left the comfort of her bed. She'd slept there long enough already. Perhaps it was the bed itself he had a dislike for?

As she approached him, a bright flush rose up his neck and into his cheeks. He kept his eyes averted, first to the floor, then to the side when she stood before him almost close enough to touch.

"Do you prefer males?" she asked, leaning up on tiptoe to whisper the question in his ear. The answer was evident from the swell in the front of his britches, but she enjoyed the irritation on his face nonetheless. It almost got him to look at her again.

His jaw muscles clenched and he shook his head curtly. "I prefer a woman I can talk to, that's all."

"And my naked body is not worthy of words?" She gazed down at herself and slid her hands over her slight curves. The touch felt nice, but not as nice as his hands might feel—his hands that were now clenched tightly by his sides. She began to slowly walk around him. When she paused in the direction his head was turned, she saw his eyes were tightly shut.

"Racha…" he began in a desperate tone. He opened his eyes finally and let his gaze rake down her length. Her nipples prickled tantalizingly when the look lingered on her breasts. His hands relaxed and he raised one up. He gently cupped her jaw and she gasped, surprised at how warm and gentle his touch was against her skin, in contrast to how rough his calloused fingertips felt. "You are worth more than a word or a touch, I'm positive. You might be worth the entire universe, but until I know more about you, this…" He swept his hand in a gesture down the length of her body. "…isn't happening."

She let out a deep sigh, expelling a cloud of thick, iridescent breath that she manipulated into a diaphanous gown to cover her naked body.

"Alright," she said, once he'd finally relaxed a bit more now that she had hidden all her best assets. "Let's sit and talk."

She sat cross-legged right where they stood and peered up at him. From a lower angle he appeared even more impressive than before. She'd liked the look of him the second he'd walked through the door, and even found his obstinacy endearing in a way. He was so very different from the male dragons she knew, all bent on their various seductions, eager and willing to devote their unflagging attentions on as many partners as possible. It became a game to most, even the females, to collect multiple lovers just to prove their prowess.

Racha tasted the Nirvana of five of the humans who had entered the temple, and the essence of the dragons who had coaxed it from them. It was power she would not keep, however, for it was the power with which she would awaken the rest of the sleeping brood that occupied the smaller chambers throughout the temple. The human man who sat before her was the key, and he seemed oblivious to the effect holding that power in check was having on her.

She could be patient for a time. She would have to, even though the scent of him had made her almost uncomfortably wet and caused the power she held to pulse insistently in her core, seeking release. Now she watched the play of the muscles beneath the fabric of his shirt when he finally bent to sit across from her, knees bent and his arms resting casually across them. It was a defensive posture, unlike her own. Even though he couldn't physically see her spread labia, the light brush of her gown over her skin made it difficult to forget how aroused she was.

"Tell me what you would like to know," she said. "I am an open book."

CHAPTER THREE

Corey felt like such a lech sitting across from Racha and struggling not to imagine how open her book might be just then. Was it some trick of the air currents in there that he could imagine the lush scent of her sex thick in his nostrils? He was at least grateful that she'd covered up, though her wispy gown left little to the imagination.

Now she sat looking attentively at him, waiting for him to speak to her, to tell her what it was he wanted to know.

He couldn't think of a damn thing to ask. All he kept thinking about was his first date with his ex and how they'd hit it off so spectacularly that they'd ended up in bed forty-five minutes later. He hadn't needed any prompting for conversation with Jill—they'd had too much in common already, including both professional and extracurricular interests. Not to mention there had been that amazing spark of attraction that he'd felt instantly when they shared a joke. He'd always been that easygoing with women. It wasn't until after she'd left him for some corporate executive only a few months later that it became pretty much impossible to carry on a conversation with another woman without instantly comparing her to Jill.

He owed this lovely young woman something.

"I'm gonna go out on a limb here and guess that you have no idea what a 'date' is, do you?" he asked.

She frowned and shook her head. "I admit I will have to reacquaint myself with human conventions, but I'm hoping you'll be the one to show me."

Corey was struck by her unassuming attitude now that they were seated across from each other, on fairly equal ground. He took a fresh look at her, trying to shed the preconception of her as a dragon queen. Her sleek, black curls were a little mussed and one of her gauzy straps had slipped off one shoulder. Her slightly slanted, almond-shaped, green eyes watched with intelligent curiosity, maybe just a little eager for him to move things along.

"We'd be having sex right now if things were going your way, wouldn't we?" he asked softly.

She lowered her dark eyelashes until they brushed the tops of her pink cheeks and nodded. "Yes. You don't understand the effort it takes to wait, but we will wait if it makes it a better experience for you."

"Tell me what it feels like…to be…like you are."

"Like a dragon? Or like the Queen of Dragons?"

He shrugged. "Both, if you want."

"You observed the others, did you not? Being a dragon is like that. Giving pleasure to as many as we can, or to one person many times. It's that energy which sustains us, allows us to do our magic. Even this gown I wear for you required energy. Maintaining this form requires energy, but it is second nature. Some of my energy is innate but not all of it. What my brother gave me does not belong to me, it belongs to the others. I must give it to them soon."

"The others…do you mean this *brood* that Kris mentioned?" Corey couldn't disguise the apprehensive tone in his voice. He still didn't quite know what to think about the idea of a multitude of magical flying, fucking creatures taking over the world as a result of what he might do today.

Racha smiled proudly. "Yes, the brood. They're my children."

"Hang on," he said, shifting backwards a couple inches. "You've gotta have a…a…*mate*, or whatever you call it to have kids, right? How many are there in this brood of yours?"

"Corey, no, they are not my blood children. We are all of the same generation. I've never mated. I've never even played at it like other young dragons do. But as Queen, I am both mentor and caretaker of all of them. I spent my early life training for this honor before I slept."

He relaxed again. "So you're like the CEO or something. Or maybe a cult leader," he muttered.

Racha laughed, the sound low and melodic. "I know of cults. It used to be a cult that we relied on to awaken past generations, but the mates from those groups made poor parents. I had the good fortune to have two dragon parents, but other dragons aren't so blessed. Luckily the imperative to breed is strong enough that most dragons have multiple mates so the dragonlings don't want for adequate role models."

"Right, and a parent dead set on fucking everything in sight is an adequate role model?" He'd seen the male dragons in the group earlier. With the exception of Hallie's Kol, who he'd actually come to respect, he found it hard to stomach how easily the others seemed to be with fucking—well, anyone. He wasn't sure if their tenderness during the act was enough to justify the promiscuity.

There was that laugh again, the sound catching his attention and holding it like his favorite song always did. It sank into his mind, calming him.

"Don't let the ritual give you the wrong impression of how we behave. Yes, sex is one of our key methods of survival, but if you could only conceive perhaps three children in a decade wouldn't you try to take advantage of every opportunity you could?" She cocked her head cutely, but the words still sank in.

"So you're telling me that the whole purpose for this ritual was to knock up all our women?" Corey could hear his voice rising in pitch and was about to run out of the room and force condoms on all the other men if he had to.

"Knock up?" She shook her head and stared at him, uncomprehending.

"Yeah, you know…*Impregnate them.*"

"Oh, Sweet Mother, no! The ritual's sole purpose is to awaken the brood. Impregnation is not possible until we leave the temple. And even then it's not guaranteed for dragons, even if their mates are willing."

"Oh." Corey deflated and the rest of what she'd said finally caught up to him. He did the math. Five hundred years, the dragons had been here. In ten years of what she suggested might be sex every bit as enthusiastic as what he'd just witnessed, they might conceive only *three* children? "Geeze, I'm sorry. How many dragons are there, anyway?"

"Several hundred. Our numbers are strictly monitored. There are never more than a thousand of us in any generation."

"Christ. I'm one of seven kids. I have about a dozen nieces and nephews, too."

Racha's eyes widened at his confession. "How many humans are there now? When we slept there were maybe a few hundred million."

"Ooh, there's a lot more of us now. A *lot* more. More than seven billion last count."

Racha froze and stared at him, her mouth working, but no words came out.

Corey relaxed, the wide-eyed wonder at what was in store for Racha giving him the upper hand for the first time. He might still have an incredible hard-on for the beauty, but seeing her flustered over the idea of how outnumbered she and her brood were at least gave him slight comfort. It didn't make him stop wanting her, though. On the contrary, it made Racha—the Queen of Dragons—even sweeter to him. Suddenly she wasn't this unusual creature who could do magic beyond his imagining, who could very likely command his cock with a twitch of a finger. Now she was just a young woman, embarking on a new life and very much out of her element.

His protector instinct kicked in and he shifted closer to her, reaching for her hands and holding them gently between his. She twitched in surprise at the sudden contact and he realized it was the first time he'd touched her.

"Shh," he said. "It's really not so bad out there. You guys seem to like having more of us anyway, right?"

She recovered quickly, but didn't remove her hands from his. Her grip tightened around his fingers and a jolt of pleasure shot between his thighs, reminding him of the perpetual hard-on he'd been sporting since the last room.

"Yes, but right now I have you. Will you show me the ways of this new world? I know human nature well enough, but conventions shift. Will you help me, Corey?"

Was it crazy of him to want to say yes? She was just a girl trying to find her way, and she needed his help. With four younger sisters he knew how thankless the task of older brother could be, but also how rewarding. Except he didn't feel particularly fraternal toward this pretty young woman.

He sensed a strength in her that his sisters never had. Something iron-hard and probably razor-tipped that kept him from giving in and trusting her. He was attracted to that glimmer of strength, but wasn't the least bit fooled by her plea.

"No, because I don't trust you." He gave her a pained expression and released her hands gently. He regretting having to disappoint her, but he had to tell her the truth. "I just can't do this. I'm sorry. I'll help if I can, but you'll just have to find someone else to do the deed."

CHAPTER FOUR

Racha stared down at the space between them where their hands had been joined. How was she supposed to make him understand? If what Corey said was true, the modern world she had awoken to was far different from the one she'd fallen asleep in, but that was the least of her concerns.

"I do need you, but not for the reasons you think." Racha reached for Corey, but his hand shot up quickly and gripped her wrist before it reached his cheek.

"No. I've seen your power. I think the only thing you need from me is a good hard fuck and after that we'll be done. Tell me, do you really want me? Or am I just some surrogate prick you can use to escape this prison?"

The strength of his grip startled her at first, but the ferocity of his gaze angered her. "Let go of me! You don't understand!"

"You're a dragon. You have power. Make me understand." His brows drew together shadowing his already dark eyes. Eyes she'd begun to get lost in while they spoke, but which now frightened her.

Frustration beat at her will as she struggled against his strong grasp. How had this man not given in to the magic already like the rest of them? "I can't force you! My magic doesn't work that way."

"I don't care how you do it. If you want me to know how badly you need me, make me understand why." His eyebrows raised in emphasis and he let go of her wrists, leaving them tingling from his touch. She wished she could go back just a few moments to better enjoy the first gentle grasp of his fingers around hers. He was a good man, but not a one to suffer secrets easily.

Racha's chest constricted with a tight, painful feeling she'd never experienced before. She stood up abruptly and walked away a pace, struggling to contain the emotions welling up. Wet droplets trailed down her cheeks and she raised a hand to wipe at one.

She stared at the crystalline orb on her fingertip, not comprehending what it meant but knowing she'd been beaten. There was no recourse. No other alternatives. If he didn't agree to their coupling there was only one thing left to do. The power was already swelling to a breaking point within her. It must be close to dawn.

She sighed shakily and nodded, still refusing to face him. "There is an alternative. The power is persistent. We are each other's slaves right now, the power and I. You would have been the key to our release. If you won't give yourself to me, the power will take its course anyway."

"What do I need to do?"

"Leave. You're safer out of this room."

"No. Tell me what to do. Let me at least help."

She turned on him, her chest tight with rage as much as sorrow. "You want to *help?* What I want more than *anything* is for you to *fuck me*. But it isn't just to release the others. I…I want you."

She wanted him like she couldn't believe—for his strength of will as much as his strong body. A man who had withstood the magic of the temple throughout the entire ritual and held out only to give her a chance at convincing him to give in would have been a perfect mate.

She cursed herself for the lack of effect her words had on him. She'd been so strong as a young dragon. She excelled at her training, was described as persuasive and effective by her teachers and the Council both. Yet this *man* somehow made cracks appear in her foundation that she'd never known existed.

He didn't answer her, just looked away again, his jaw clenching. If he wouldn't have her, and wouldn't leave either, there was only one other option.

"I want you to bind me before it's too late. The power will force me to change and I may not be rational when it takes over. If you insist on staying, you must bind me or I can't promise you'll survive until dawn."

She held her tongue on the last plea she could have given him that may have changed his mind, but to tell him now would only make her seem weak and helpless. She would not end this night by begging.

CHAPTER FIVE

Corey's chest burned, the conflicting emotions warring inside him. Yes, he wanted Racha but that wasn't enough to compromise his principles. In another time, perhaps he might have gone through with it but not now. Not after everything he'd been through with Jill, then the failures with women after her. He was grateful Erika had seemed to see that damaged part of him and steer clear in spite of their attraction. Hallie had tried, but both of them had known it wasn't meant to be.

Racha shot one last beseeching look at him, her bright green eyes brimming with tears, then nodded and turned toward the bed.

Somehow Corey knew the tears were real, and not some ploy to manipulate him into changing his mind. Why did that understanding make him suddenly feel like crying, too? He could do this thing she asked. Bind her to her bed and try to give her some comfort through her ordeal. Company was something he could offer her, at least.

He followed her, watching the sway of her hips and the ripple of her gauzy gown where it draped alluringly over her slight curves. Abstractly he thought a woman more perfect for him probably couldn't exist, at least in terms of features he preferred. Petite and beautiful, with just the right amount of muscle mass relative to soft curves. He could easily picture gripping her round bottom while she rode him and those intense green eyes looking into his, her dark-lashed eyelids fluttering with pleasure while he…

Get her out of your head, man. You don't even know her!

Maybe after he got her through this they could talk more. Maybe something *could* work out for them both. It was just way too soon for him to lose his mind over a woman because of sex. He wanted a clear head when he decided whether or not he could love her.

Her skin seemed to pulse with a luminescent internal glow as she crawled onto the bed and lay down in the center.

Corey had to climb on after her to reach her. He did his best not to look at her while he found the ropes that were already fastened to the green jade columns of the bedposts.

Racha silently raised her arms. When Corey stole a glance at her face, her eyes were closed, her cheeks still streaked with tears.

"How long will this take?" he asked in a gentle voice. The rope slid silkily through his fingers as he secured one of her wrists deftly in a sailor's knot, then moved to tie the other.

"I don't know. I think it happens instantly when the sun rises, but I can feel the power pushing to get free already."

Corey glanced at his watch. Sunrise was only a short while off, by his calculations.

"Should I tie your feet, too?"

"Yes."

"What does it feel like?" he asked while binding her ankles to the other two bedposts.

She let out a soft moan and shimmers of pale light traced up the skin of her feet and legs where Corey held them. The barest texture of greenish scales was visible as the light traveled up her lower legs.

"It feels pleasurable sometimes, but others…" Racha's words halted with a strangled cry and her back arched violently, limbs straining at her bindings. Her free foot kicked away from his grip and Corey barely managed to dodge it before it smacked into his jaw. He gripped her ankle and quickly secured it with the rope.

Corey moved up beside her once the spasms subsided.

Racha lay panting, her chest heaving from the exertion. Her brow shimmered with green-tinged sweat.

"Shh," Corey said. "I'm with you. I won't leave you until it's over, I promise."

Racha gave him a weak smile that disappeared when another ripple of light passed across her skin. Her lips parted and her brow creased as though she were bracing herself for the next painful episode.

The spasm began and she let out a strangled cry. The sound rose in strength, becoming a deafening roar incongruous with the petite form it escaped from.

At a loss for what to do, Corey rested one large hand against her shoulder and squeezed in an effort at comfort. Her skin felt feverish to the touch.

The bed shook and her skin rippled not only with light but with undulating waves of motion.

The barely there slip of a gown she wore faded away like dissipating fog. Translucent green scales replaced it, covering her arms, legs, and torso. Only her creamy-white breasts remained bare and pristine with small, erect pink nipples.

Her body collapsed back against the bed, limp and panting.

Corey slid closer to her and carefully leaned on one elbow so her cheek rested against his chest. With his free hand he brushed sweat-drenched curls off her brow and caressed her temple.

"You'll be alright." Impulsively he bent and pressed his lips against her forehead.

"T-tell Kris that he and Issa have my blessing." She slurred the words out in between harsh pants to regain her breath.

He kept ahold of her through the next series of seizures that wracked her body from head to toe.

"Tell them yourself when this is over" he said gruffly. He was so tense with worry for her he'd entirely forgotten the previously persistent discomfort from hours of aching arousal. In fact, he was pretty sure his cock had gone on vacation.

Her fever grew with each body-wrenching spasm. During the next one, large, coiling green horns emerged from her forehead and tangled up with her curly, sweat-drenched black locks. Her eyes glowed with green fire and a green, forked tongue darted out to lick her dry lips.

Tears streamed unchecked down her cheeks and Corey reached up to brush them away with a thumb.

She shook her head, nearly delirious. "Corey, thank you for staying. You would have been a fine mate. I am sorry."

Her words had the weight of the words of a person in the throes of death. Corey struggled to suppress an irrational panic that solidified like an icy stone in his belly. She hadn't said what would happen, had she?

"Do I need to get Kris? Can someone else help?" He feebly grasped at ideas. Something wasn't right, but she hadn't told him anything. He had been right not to trust her, but for the wrong reasons.

Her green gaze latched onto his, wide and terrified, but also resigned to her fate. Her entire body shook against her restraints.

"The energy will consume me alive like this. But it was…the only other way to give it to them. They must awaken. If I have no release by my mate's touch, the power will still find a way out. It is my burden…and my honor."

"No! There has to be some other way!" Had it really come to this, because of his own ridiculous sense of propriety? What a goddamned hypocrite he was, too. *Yeah, man, when the dragon queen asks you to fuck, you say, "How hard?"*

Racha shook her head. "Too late…" she murmured in a weak voice just before another spasm gripped her body, forcing her head and feet to dig into the bed and her torso to torque violently.

He'd been such a fool not to read the signs. The resignation, her nearly exhausted look when he tied her, the tears. She wasn't such a weak woman to give in to rejection by crying. Her tears had meant something completely different, and the understanding chilled him to the bone.

The light from beneath her skin became nearly blinding, pulsing from every velvet scale. Corey hurriedly stripped and waited for her body to sink back to the bed again.

"God help me," he said. He hoped it wasn't too late for her. She had said she would shift, and the transformation was clearly occurring, but had only gone partway so far if what he'd seen the other dragons do was any indication. Perhaps there was still time if he hurried.

When she relaxed again he wasted no time.

He pressed his mouth to hers, tenderly at first, then harder when a moan escaped her lips and she raised her head to kiss him back. The wet velveteen sensation of her alien tongue filled his mouth. Within only a few seconds he was rock hard again.

He pulled away, breathless, whispering, "I'm sorry. Why didn't you tell me it would kill you?"

Her nipples had become a verdant shade of green, but the color didn't faze him now. Not the way their hard, pebbly texture felt on his tongue.

"Please don't stop," she gasped, her chest now arching up to meet the teasing suck of his mouth on her breasts. Fuck, she tasted amazing. Refreshing to his heated arousal, in spite of how much hotter her skin was under his tongue. He had no time to pause and savor her now, though.

Corey cursed himself for tying her. Had he just known… what would he have done? Bedded her in a more proper way while still resenting the fact of doing it? Taken his selfish time to gain his own pleasure from her body?

Now he had no choice—make her come or watch her die, likely in a brilliant show of fireworks that would rival Kris's.

"Racha, baby. I've got you. I'm going to fuck you now. You'll be okay soon."

He pressed fingers between her spread thighs. The wet heat that he encountered sent his head spinning. She was slick and ready and so hot.

Her bindings made the position less than ideal, but she tilted her hips up into his touch as far as she could. He met her desperate gaze as he moved to lay atop her, holding his weight off her body with one arm while he used the free hand to guide his throbbing tip between her folds.

"Please hurry," she said through green-tinged lips. The telltale surge of illumination began to glow beneath her skin again, beginning at the tips of her horns and running southward.

She is even lovelier like this, he thought as he slid deep inside her with one quick thrust.

Racha's head pressed back against the pillows and she cried out.

She's a virgin, you asshole!

Corey hesitated for a split second until he saw the slight smile on her lips that widened just a bit when he pulled back out slowly. He thrust again, more gently the second time, then again, encouraged by her soft sigh and the press of her naked torso up against him.

His body rejoiced at the sensations of her skin against his, her tight sheathe gripping his cock while he buried it over and over inside her. Yet this wasn't about his pleasure now. While he knew the tricks of many women's bodies, he'd never been with this particular beautiful young woman. She felt more heavenly beneath him than anyone else in memory. Would her body have the same response to him as his did to her?

Sensing her urgency from the intent look on her face, he reached between them and pressed his fingers against the swollen nub between her thighs.

After just a few circular strokes, she cried out and her slick muscles tightened around his cock. The intense squeeze of her overwhelmed him and he struggled not to lose his pumping rhythm before she was ready. It was an effort to hold back, but he didn't to restrain himself for long.

At that moment, she arched her chest into him and let out a harsh, gasping cry. The light within her coalesced into a hot, white ball of ecstasy between them. It grew in brightness and intensity until it encompassed them both.

An electric buzz seemed to pass through Corey. He lost strength in his arms and almost fell atop her. At the last second he reached up and gripped her hands above her bindings, entwining his fingers with hers while they rode the currents of power that rocketed through them, pushing ever outward.

The heat of it reached searing proportions. The resonance of a singing chime filled Corey's head as intense as both their cries. Electric vibrations coursed through his body, from the point where they were joined to every extremity. Visual pulses of light shot out from them both and he could feel each one taking a piece of him with it. He was about to die here with her, from the pleasure of her contact and the explosive release of his soul in one complete and glorious moment. And he had no regrets. Not even this. Especially not this.

Just when he believed the power would tear them both apart, it exploded, the energy rolling out and away from them, surging through the walls of the chamber and making everything it its path glow and pulse with power in rhythm with their own orgasms.

With the departure of all that immense power went the remains of Corey's own energy. Nothing was left behind but two sweating bodies, their panting breaths echoing starkly in the chamber.

Corey struggled for a moment to keep himself up. He had just long enough to look into Racha's eyes to ensure her continued consciousness. He was incapable of speech himself, but hoped his own expression would convey the magnitude of what they had just shared.

When their gazes met, he registered an expression of unrestrained gratitude, before he finally gave in and collapsed, breathless, beside her.

CHAPTER SIX

The exhaustion Racha felt in the aftermath was a welcome respite from the intense pressure of the power that had finally been released. She still wanted more of Corey, however, but knew it might not be possible. He had only done what he had to save her life. She was grateful, and would find some way to reward him, but it wouldn't be in the manner she had always dreamed.

She clenched her eyes shut tightly, struggling to hold back more tears. She'd already cried enough in his presence and refused to now, even though the departure of his thick, hard length from inside her had left her feeling every bit as empty as the absence of the power.

But she was alive, at least. The elated murmur of hundreds of dragon voices reached out to her in diffident gratitude. That was reward enough. It would have to be.

Dimly she became aware of gentle tugging at her wrists, then her ankles. She opened her eyes when Corey was at her feet and watched in open admiration at the flex of his broad shoulders while he untied her, then tossed the bindings across the room in disgust.

He ran large, shaky fingers through thick, tousled brown hair. He looked as beaten down and exhausted as she felt, but seemed to gather himself together with a deep breath. She braced herself for what he would say when he turned to her.

He said nothing, at first. He just turned and knelt between her ankles, raised one foot to his thigh and rubbed the skin gently where the rope had dug into it. It was tender, but the skin wasn't broken and his warm, calloused touch felt nice. It felt even nicer when his large palm slid higher, skimming up her smooth calf.

Racha tried to pull away from his grip and rise, but he held her ankle tight.

"Hey, pretty dragon lady," he said with a smile. "You just stay put a little while, alright?"

"You don't have to. You did what I needed you to do. You can go now."

Corey frowned and picked up her other foot, beginning the slow, delicious massaging again.

"No, I can't. You see, I'm the kind of guy who sticks around. I'm also the kind who pays attention and I've been watching the rest of this crew all night—well, most of them, anyway. One thing I noticed is that at the end of each little *phase*, all of my friends were given a sort of…well…gift."

"I won't mark you if you don't want me to." She knew what she offered was against Dragon Law, but there were always extenuating circumstances during awakenings. Concessions would be made.

Corey shook his head and narrowed his eyes at her. His hands continued their tender caresses, now along the skin above her left knee. His touch sent pleasant tingles straight between her legs. He shifted his hands so that both palms skimmed down her inner thighs.

"If you want me to trust you, Racha, you need to start spilling your secrets. I'm pretty sure those little tattoos the rest of my team got are damn important to you all, or the other dragons wouldn't have wasted so little time doling them out. Tell me what they mean to you and why you didn't give me one."

Racha closed her eyes. Her mind churned over how to tell him. She didn't want to bind a man to her who didn't want her, but she feared he would accept her mark out of some sense of obligation. Just like he'd finally given in and helped her release the power.

She'd survived the awakening. Perhaps the Council would understand if she failed to mark him. They could let Corey find another female more to his liking and send Racha a mate who was willing.

She gasped when his fingertips reached her core and teased along her lips, still wet from their combined juices. He sank his fingers into her slowly, then drew them back out again and teased around her clit in tortuous, slow circles. Even though he'd untied her, she was too mesmerized by his touch to move away.

When he pulled his hand away after a second, her hips raised up on their own, seeking contact.

"Please," she whispered. "I need more of you."

In truth, she was depleted of all but the barest wisp of power now. If he would only bury himself in her again and give her more, perhaps she could think of the right answers.

"More of this?" He leaned down beside her and flicked his tongue over her nipple while his fingers moved back between her thighs, caressing just enough to make her crave more, but not giving it to her.

"Yes, more!"

"Answer my question first. Why didn't you mark me?"

Just when her throbbing need had subsided and she thought she could regain her senses, he began again. He thrust his fingers deeper and teased her clit so expertly she thought she might just lose control. Except he stopped again.

She nearly cried out in frustration until she felt a hot, hard pressure pulse against her hip. Her eyes flew open and she looked at him.

He gazed down at her, a fevered expression on his face. He looked almost haggard with longing.

Experimentally, she shifted her hips slightly so that she rubbed against him.

Corey's eyelids fluttered and fell shut. His hand came to rest on her mound again, fingers gently stroking as before.

"You still want me?" she whispered.

His voice came out in a rough growl. "Like nothing I've wanted in my life." His eyes opened again and he met her gaze.

In those brown depths she saw the truth of his words, and it shattered her. The tears began again, only this time they weren't from sorrow or regret.

She sat up abruptly and captured his mouth with hers.

Corey tried to push her back, a mumbled objection making it to her ears, but she pushed harder, forcing him back against her pillows. He went, pulling her with him.

She kept kissing him, peppering his face, his neck, his chest with more kisses, elated at finally understanding. Once she let him have his breath and had moved down his torso, he let out a low, frustrated grumble.

"You gonna answer my question?"

She only nodded and smiled up at him from between his legs. She would answer all his questions, but first she needed more of him.

His hard shaft was coated with the flavor of them both. She savored every inch when she slipped her mouth over his tip and down, licking and sucking as she went.

"Oh, fuck, baby. You're driving me crazy. Do you…" He seemed intent on saying more, but the rest only came out as a strangled groan when his hips rose up off the bed in a violent jerk.

His orgasm flooded her tongue as sweetly as the power it carried into her with his abating pleasure. The sweet rush of his Nirvana invigorated her, cleared her mind and conscience, and left nothing behind but the exultation of being with him and knowing he was not unwilling as she had believed a few moments earlier.

She crawled back up his body and lay fully atop his panting chest.

He gazed up at her, a perplexed and slightly irritated smile on his face that disappeared as he let out a hearty laugh.

"That was nice. More than nice. But you're not off the hook that easily," he said.

"I am an open book," she said with a grin.

Then she explained everything.

He held her tightly and buried his face against her neck when she stopped talking.

"Are you angry?" she asked.

"God, no. I just…Racha, you could have died before I ever got a chance to learn how good this feels. That thought terrifies me."

He suddenly flipped her over and kissed her roughly. His resurging erection pressed hot and hard against her belly.

She laughed. "What are you doing?"

"Forgive me. I just need to make love to you again. Gotta make extra sure you won't self-destruct."

Racha pushed back against him and sat up when he leaned back on his heels.

"What is it?" he asked.

"There is just one thing I need to do first, if you're willing. Are you?"

CHAPTER SEVEN

*A*m I willing to be hers. Marked. Branded. Bonded? Corey's mind ran through all the things she'd told him the mark meant. She admitted she hadn't told him everything, just what mattered.

He'd always imagined the day he would ask a woman to marry him. He'd get down on one knee, hand her a ring after saying something particularly eloquent that he could never have thought up himself. There might be music playing and champagne. And ideally they'd have been together long enough that he knew all her secrets well enough that there would be no surprises.

This isn't the same thing, by a longshot, he told himself. But somehow it was. Commitment wasn't something he was shy about. Hell, he'd come on this expedition, hadn't he?

Yet every moment of this expedition had been a surprise and Racha was just the cherry on top. Fate was telling him something and maybe, for once, he ought to listen.

Corey looked down at the petite beauty, finally letting himself hear what it was fate wanted for him. He answered her question with a kiss, tongue sliding deep. Every ounce of hesitation or reluctance disappeared with the stroke of her tongue against his.

He spent a second vaguely aware that when they kissed her tongue felt as solid and fleshy as a human tongue. As human as all the rest of her now that the power had ebbed and her skin had regained its normal pink sheen.

Except this is not normal for her. What I saw before is closer to what she is. The idea didn't bother him as much as it might have the day before. On the contrary, it made him want her more.

He held still while she traced her lips down over his jaw and throat, closing his eyes at the silken caress of her lips and tongue. She paused at his chest and pulled back. A gentle fingertip traced a large pattern on his pec just over his left nipple, leaving a tingling sensation behind.

Corey looked down just as she darted her forked tongue out to redraw the same pattern with swift, stinging strokes. The sting didn't bother him any more than any of his other tattoos had. Nor did the understanding of what it meant. She had explained that the glowing magic that infused the mark protected him, and established their bond—one that would not be broken until one of them died.

The gravity of the small ritual hit him when she gazed up into his eyes. Her fingertips dug a little harder into his naked thighs. She seemed to be waiting for his reaction. He didn't feel any different, however. The abiding need to be with her hadn't changed, only now it was accompanied by a sense of permanence. Far from frightening, the feeling was a comfort.

"You're what I've always wanted," he said.

Racha raised up on her knees and wrapped her arms around him. He embraced her and carried her back down to the bed with him. Even the sounds she made were perfect little breathy moans as he explored her body with mouth and hands.

Her fingers tangled in his hair when he lowered his head between her thighs for the first time, tongue flicking out, eager to taste the sweet place his cock had been deeply buried in earlier. She spread her legs wider and tilted her hips up to meet the thrust of his tongue deep into the hot, velvet depths of her. His head buzzed from the tangy flavor and heady aroma of her sex. He had to taste the flood of her climax before he made love to her again.

She writhed and cried out when she came and Corey braced himself for a violent, spectacular surge of energy, but all that happened was exactly what he'd hoped—the drenched folds of her pussy spasmed against his lips, coating them with even more of her sweet flavor. He lapped it up, ignoring the giddy twitches and stuttering breath from her until he'd had his fill.

"Are you ready for more?" he asked, rising up onto his knees and gripping her hips. He tugged her toward him until his hard cock slid against her well-attended pussy. He smiled when her eyes rolled back and she nodded.

With a slow, deliberate thrust, he buried himself deep into her. He fucked her as slowly as he could endure, watching her face with each stroke to gauge where she found the most pleasure. She quickly reached the point of quivering, pent-up need for release again.

"Touch yourself," he said gruffly, pushing her legs a little wider and hooking her thighs over his arms.

She gave him a fleeting smile in acknowledgment before her face drifted back to a mask of pure enjoyment. Her fingers slipped between her thighs and Corey groaned at the way she gripped him at first, squeezing the base of his cock while he pistoned into her.

Her gorgeous, small breasts thrust up when she arched her back in response to the first touch of her fingers on her clit. She rubbed in tight little circles, obviously adept at pleasuring herself, but seemed to lose rhythm the deeper and harder he fucked her.

He sucked first one pert nipple into his mouth until she moaned, then the other. The tight squeeze of her pussy became more than he could endure.

Her hips bucked hard into his. He yelled out her name and bent over her, fucking with an erratic, pumping rhythm while his climax gripped him. The shuddering pull of her muscles surrounded his cock and milked him dry.

The glow that accompanied her climax was subtle at first, then grew brighter, coursing through her in tiny ripples across her skin. He watched, enthralled until it subsided and her eyes opened. She gave him a sleepy smile.

"You're glowing," he said.

"So are you." She gestured at the mark on his chest. He looked down to see that it was, indeed, glowing with a faint, green light.

"Does this happen every time?"

"Now that the ritual is finished, when we please each other like that, we share our energy. You give me your Nirvana and I give back some of my magic. It protects you. It also reminds other dragons that you belong to me."

"Oh?" he asked with a cock of one eyebrow. "And who in their right mind would steal from the Queen? Not that I'd go with anyone else, of course."

"No one would, but the mark will ensure you're treated with the level of respect deserved of the Queen's Consort."

Consort. Corey let the title roll around in his head, not sure how he should feel about it. It sounded a little fancy for a guy raised by a traditional, blue-collar family like he had been. He brushed it off as yet another old convention her kind had that they'd learn to outgrow once they acquainted themselves with the modern world. But if the mark gave him an advantage over other dragons, that was a good thing, right?

A thought occurred to him. "So what's to remind other people…or dragons that you belong to *me*?"

She tilted her chin at his chest again. "That mark means I'm yours. Dragons can bond with many humans, but many of us choose only a few as true mates. Some only choose one—the fewer we choose, the stronger our bond is."

She seemed to grow a little pensive and turned away from him, burying her head in her pillow.

"Well that's good, right? We both got pretty lucky, I think." He lay down beside her and brushed his palm down her back.

"It depends on what the world is like out there now and if you can endure a lifetime with me."

"Hey, what's this talk of enduring? I'm in this for the long haul. The world's mostly pretty great. Confusing as fuck a lot of times, but you're a bright girl, you'll get the hang of it."

She turned back to meet his gaze, her lips pursed. "I'm not concerned about adjusting to your world. It's you adjusting to *our* world that worries me. "

Something niggled at the back of his mind as he attempted to comfort her, though. The whole *lifetime* thing.

"Wait, you've been asleep in here for how long? Five hundred years?"

She nodded solemnly.

"So, when you say 'lifetime' how long are we talking?"

She eyed the mark on his chest again. "My magic…. As long as I share it with you, you will live as long as I do."

Corey narrowed his eyes at her evasive answer. "Spit it out, Racha."

"Another five hundred years, give or take."

He leaned back and stared at the ceiling. "'Give or take,' she says," he muttered. "What about the others?" he asked, looking at her again.

"It works the same for them, though the more mates they collect, the shorter their lifespans. Some consider it worth the sacrifice, others don't."

Corey had never in a million years considered he'd walk away from this expedition with such a confounding gift. But it sounded like she was hedging on something.

"What aren't you telling me?"

"It means we are bound together for the duration. Some mates can't endure it. After the first century they go a little mad. Some commit suicide rather than go on."

"So, we can still die…"

"Yes. Did you think we were immortal?"

"Well, from my perspective it sure seemed that way. But wow…Imagine the things you can see in five hundred years."

Racha grimaced. "My mother told me it was easier living in the monastery. The world was cruel when I was a child, and crueler still during the lifetime before Mother awoke. She always said it never changed much between generations."

Corey tried to recall all he knew of ancient history. Half a millennium ago wasn't precisely the dark ages, but it may as well have been from his perspective. She was going to be over-whelmed by the changes, and he was only too eager to show them all to her and see how she reacted.

"Everything moves a lot quicker now than it did when you were young."

"But you weren't even there, how do you know?"

"Erika and the others can tell you—it's their specialty, not mine. All I know is that in *this* lifetime, two people can speak to each other instantly from opposite sides of the planet, and it takes about a day to travel that far. But humans haven't changed all that much. We still eat and shit and fuck. We fall in love and we make babies and we try to raise them to be like us and fail miserably. My point is, the world is changing faster than even I can comprehend right now, but at the same time it's all the same. Having centuries to absorb it all could be a lot of fun. Especially with the right person."

Racha smiled at him. "I'm glad it was you who came into my chamber today."

"So am I," he said, laying a kiss upon the swell of her creamy breast.

She rose abruptly and with a breath was pristinely coifed and clad in a much more solid piece of clothing than she'd worn for him earlier. If it were possible, she looked even more stunning.

"Where are you going?" he asked.

"It's time to meet the brood. You should dress. I can hear their eagerness to leave—they are already assembling in the Grand Hall."

Corey grabbed her hand before she could walk away.

"No matter what happens, I'm with you," he said.

"Thank you."

CHAPTER EIGHT

The excitement in the huge hall was infectious. Erika stood near the front of the Queen's dais, as giddy with the mood as the rest of them. She stared around, marveling at all the beautiful figures that filled up the tiers that surrounded them.

"Geva, I had no idea there were so many of you!"

Her lover's arms wrapped around her waist and his lips brushed her ear. "We are all here thanks to you and your friends. I will spend the rest of my life thanking you for your sacrifice."

She snorted out a laugh. "Sacrifice? With that tongue of yours, I promise, the pleasure was *all* mine."

The other members of her team had gathered around, standing before the dais that held the throne. Waiting.

"What do you think is taking them so long?" Hallie whispered.

"I bet they fell in love like I did," Camille said, eyes twinkling. Erika eyed the pretty blonde where she stood flanked by the two beautiful men who couldn't take their hands off her. Even now, Eben was stroking her back and Roka held her hand, pulling it up to his lips and kissing it periodically.

All the dragons had foregone their preferred nudity in favor of garments in every color. Erika admired the man at her side. How sexy would he look in modern clothes if he cleaned up this nice? What he wore now mimicked her own attire of loose-fitting shirt and draw-string linen pants—the cleanest things she had packed for the expedition. Geva had admitted that he could clothe her with his magic but refused to because he'd rather keep her naked.

Kris and Issa stood off to the side, sharing private whispers. Erika nudged Geva in the ribs with her elbow. "Use your fancy mental skills to ask what's taking them so long."

Geva let out a suffering sigh that would normally have provoked a deeper dig into a man's ribs from her, but the smile on his face let Erika know he enjoyed it. He grew quiet for a moment.

"Kris says they're on their way. And…No, I shouldn't say."

"The hell you say. Tell me!"

Geva grinned. "And he says the Queen sounds very happy and satisfied. Your friend Corey performed wonders, it sounds like."

Erika was on the verge of retorting when the doors behind the dais opened, and the pair emerged. Corey looked tired but radiantly happy…happier than she'd ever seen the good-natured tech. On his arm was the loveliest woman Erika had ever seen. Erika gaped for a second before realizing that everyone around her had fallen to their knees and bowed their heads. *Holy shit! Right. I'm in the presence of royalty.*

"What the hell?" Corey whispered, the words just barely audible to Erika's ears when they all knelt.

"Everyone, please stand."

The Queen's voice was strong and light and carried audibly through the room. Erika liked her already.

When all were standing again, the Queen introduced herself.

"I am Rachasara, your Queen, whom most of you already know. This is Corey." She paused to grasp Corey's hand and gaze up at him admiringly. Erika raised an eyebrow. The man did have skills if he'd made her that happy.

The Queen continued. "He tells me the changes between our birth time and this time are very drastic. Our transition may take more time than past generations experienced, but our awakening decree remains unchanged."

Erika heard murmurs of surprise and excitement and turned to look behind her. The Queen continued talking, but Erika was too fascinated—and possibly too exhausted—to focus on her words, instead becoming distracted by the activity of the other dragons. Corey had his camera on, at least, though she expected none of their footage from the last twenty-four hours would ever see the public eye.

Geva's hand clutched her hip, urging her attention back to the front.

The Queen stood before her, arms outstretched. Corey was behind her, rubbing his neck in embarrassment.

"She wanted to meet you first," he said apologetically.

"Of course!" Erika grasped the outstretched hands affectionately. The woman had startling, slanted green eyes and a sweet, heart-shaped face.

"Corey says you are the one to thank for the awakening. I am eternally grateful to you." The Queen cast a sidelong look at Geva who had seemed to recede a bit behind Erika. "Any favor you ask, I will be happy to fulfill. Even for him."

"Um, thank you so much, your highness. I hope we can talk a bit less…formally soon. I have a lot to ask you."

The Queen smiled. "Call me Racha, and I would very much like to talk." She gave Erika's hands another squeeze with her tiny, delicate fingers before moving on to speak affectionately to Kris.

"What the hell was that about?" she asked Geva who had moved back to her side.

"I told you I was a bad boy. She only knows me by reputation, so I didn't take it personally."

"Well, good to know she's forgiven you, I guess."

Geva shrugged, the overtly careless, nonchalant gesture more of an indication of his self-consciousness in the presence of his *liege* than any words could be.

"You feel *bad* about what you did, don't you?" Erika asked.

"Yes," he said, meeting her eyes squarely. "I would give anything to redeem myself. I don't feel worthy of *you* with that hanging on my past."

"Jesus, you fool. That was centuries ago! I don't care! And I get the feeling she's giving you a clean slate, too. So take advantage of it. Be better. Or just be very, very bad with me and me alone." She gave him a wicked grin, enjoying the growl and hungry kiss she got in return.

His erection was pure and present against her hip, but Erika got the sense that right here and now, amid the entire congregation, as it were, was not the place for them to indulge themselves. And the truth was, she very much looked forward to having Geva in her own domain for a change. Maybe tied to her bed in her apartment in Boston. She wondered how well her old bed could withstand the weight of a dragon. Or maybe she'd open up her family's estate again to give them more room and sturdier furnishings.

Her pulse picked up thinking about revisiting the place where she'd grown up. Particularly her father's study where she had first found the glimmer of a clue that a race like Geva's might even exist.

It was done, she realized. The last twenty-four hours had been a whirlwind. Had it really only been that long? Her watch, which she'd recovered from the pile of clothing in the first chamber when she dressed, told her that it was barely even dawn, and they'd arrived just after sunrise the day before.

Now there was a multitude of very much living and breathing dragons milling around the room. The excitement was infectious.

"What happens now?" she asked Geva, but he'd left her side again. She looked around for him, and found him and the other Court dragons standing in the center of the room.

The eight beautiful figures joined hands in a circle and raised their arms above their heads. The air above them began to shimmer. All heads in the room tilted back to observe.

Erika felt hands grip her own from either side, but her companions remained silent, as awed as she was at what was transpiring.

Before their eyes, the huge, round dome of the ceiling glowed orange as though with the breaking dawn. Waves of light hit it from beneath.

In unison, the eight figures walked backward, drawing the circle of light wider and wider until their circle encompassed the entire ceiling. Then they began to shift. Their clothing disappeared and their bodies grew. Colored scales replaced human skin. Horns coiled from graceful, elongated heads. Thick tails extended from the ends of their spines.

A moment later, eight horned heads craned up, breaths swirling together in a twisting cyclone of colorful fog. Erika's skin tingled, whether from the crackling magic in the air or simple exhilaration, she couldn't be sure. Either way, it was a spectacular sight, particularly seeing Geva's breathtaking true shape at full size.

The column of variegated smoke reached the dome and exploded in a burst of light.

When the spots receded from Erika's vision, the view above was of a clear morning sunrise, wisps of clouds still tinged pink but beginning to glow brighter each second.

The entire hall erupted in a flurry of roars and beating wings as the dragons that filled it shifted and ascended. Free for the first time in centuries.

Erika's hands were numb from the tight grips of Hallie and Camille, her vision blurry from the tears that streamed down her face.

"Beautiful," someone murmured, and she was dimly aware it was her own voice.

The others moved away while Erika still gazed up, enraptured at the sight of all those majestic horned, winged creatures taking flight.

"It is time, my love," a deep, resonant voice said.

A gust of warm breath against her neck brought her back to the present. Geva's massive, horned head took up her entire field of vision. He cocked sideways to gaze at her through one eye.

"Time for what?"

"Time to fly. Climb on."

Destiny. It had never meant anything to Erika even though it had drawn her to this expedition from the very beginning. That first day in her father's study, finding his sketches of the creatures he was sure existed but none of his colleagues would believe in. It all made sense now. This was where she belonged.

Well, maybe not *here*, in the literal sense. She looked around the austere but comfortable room she and Geva had been given at the monastery the dragons had flown to in their exodus from the temple. The trip had been both spectacular and terrifying, clinging to Geva's back while her team followed suit with the rest of the Court.

They'd finally landed on an island that had to be somewhere in the South China Sea if her sense of direction was still working. A throng of monks prostrated themselves in greeting to all the dragons, this time, not just the Queen and her retinue.

But what happened after they left this place? *Destiny,* her irritating inner voice said again. So, she believed it, and she did kinda give them all the benefit of the doubt. Particularly when one big, red dragon was insistently pulling her into a white-sheeted bed and tearing off the clothes she'd quickly thrown on to meet the Queen. *A bed. Yes, a bed would be good.*

Oh, Jesus, none of that mattered when his cock was fucking her. Dragon fucking *magic*. Followed by the pleasant burn of her tattoo and basking in the glow…a literal glow, she realized. That was new, but somehow not the least bit surprising.

Geva murmured against her sweaty skin. "We may be here for awhile, until each of the dragons is sent home. But if you can endure a wait like this, so can I. I don't really care where we are. I just want to love you for the rest of my natural life."

"Which means dragging me along for the next few centuries?" They'd had the conversation already but Erika still felt overwhelmed by the thought of being held in these arms every night for what seemed like an eternity for her.

"Yes. And others, if they're willing. It doesn't just have to be *me* who you endure. I'm sure we can find someone else equally irritating to distract you."

She laughed, but the prospect encouraged her. She loved him. Christ, it was crazy, but she did. Yet, was it so bad that she couldn't imagine five hundred years fucking one man? But if there were more of them, would she even want to share? Or even be shared?

"Why are you so tense?" he asked, massaging her shoulders. "I'm trying to make love to you but you keep me on the outside. I don't understand."

"No, you don't. Because you're not like us!" She cringed over her outburst. She'd never been quite so tied up in knots over her feelings for a man at the same time as wanting him to fuck her until she ached from head to toe. Again.

"I am more like you than you know. Let me in, sweet Erika."

He nuzzled at her breasts and she opened her legs reflexively because she really, *really* wanted him between them.

"Stop. I need to talk." She gripped his forehead just as he was about to sink his sweet tongue into her pussy. God, what a force of will *that* took.

He sat back and looked at her expectantly.

"Sweetie, you are too perfect for words. When we're done with this conversation I promise you can fuck me any way you'd like to."

Geva grinned wickedly. "So good deeds still garner rewards in this generation?"

"Yes. Yes they do. But I need to figure out how the hell we're going to support your fucking *brood* once we get out there. I can't abide homeless dragons in Boston. And they all seem so…sex starved and destitute. I mean, no offense, but the first place we come to all the residents have taken vows of poverty. Frankly, I worry for the population."

Geva's brows creased and he nodded sagely. Then let out a hearty laugh.

"You're worried we can't support ourselves?"

"Well…yeah?"

He gripped her shoulders and pushed her back against the pillows.

"My love, we are dragons. Riches are our specialty and we have cultivated them for several thousand years. We want for nothing. And neither should you. You will soon see. Yes, the humans who live here want no riches, but that is because it is their mandate to protect *our* interests. Different sects of their order have functioned in this capacity for millennia." He looked around their room with a creased brow. "They've changed since I first visited before sleeping, however. It's much cleaner now."

"So where is 'home' for these dragons? Another halfway house as destitute as this one?" Erika felt a little bad for being so pissy at him. The truth was the first meal they'd been served had been one of the most delicious dishes she'd tasted, and the bed they were in was a far cry from sleeping on hard ground.

"I said you will see. We all are descendents of the most prominent dragon citizens. These men are the keymasters to our treasure, between generations. You had a father, yes? You've spoken of him."

"Yes. I loved my dad."

"When he died, what happened to his treasure?"

She had no idea where he was going with his line of questioning but answered. "It's mine now."

"And what are you doing with it?"

"Well…nothing. I've been away too long to bother. Everything's locked up tight. Waiting for me to come home, I guess…"

She was lying a little bit. Her father's estate wasn't locked up exactly. The staff still lived there and kept it up. When she was stateside she called regularly to talk to the caretaker, Walt. Conversations were as much about her life as they were about the continued smooth running of the estate. Her father had left her enough money to keep it going for at least her lifetime, if not longer. Maybe she had been away too long?

She rolled over and looked up into Geva's eyes. "I get it. You guys all have a legacy. Lucky bunch you are, I have to say. I wonder what happens to orphaned dragons."

Geva's brow creased in confusion. "Orphans. Rare enough, but they happen. They're provided for."

Erika thought he seemed a little uncertain about his answer, but dismissed it. She wanted to ask him more, but got a little distracted by his exquisite tongue finding its way between her thighs yet again.

Yeah, she could deal with that for a few centuries, and who cared about the rest of the world?

ABOUT OPHELIA BELL

Ophelia Bell loves a good bad-boy and especially strong women in her stories. Women who aren't apologetic about enjoying sex and bad boys who don't mind being with a woman who's in charge, at least on the surface, because pretty much anything goes in the bedroom.

Ophelia grew up on a rural farm in North Carolina and now lives in Los Angeles with her own tattooed bad-boy husband and four attention-whoring cats.

You can contact her at any of the following locations:

Website: http://opheliabell.com/

Facebook: https://www.facebook.com/OpheliaDragons

Twitter: @OpheliaDragons

Goodreads: https://www.goodreads.com/OpheliaBell